To Ulla Danielsson, with thanks for the help

J. A.

Rabén & Sjögren Stockholm

Text and illustrations copyright © 1986 by Jens Ahlbom
Translation copyright © 1987 by Barbara Lucas
All rights reserved
Library of Congress catalog card number: 87-45161
Originally published in Swedish under the title *Jonatan på Måsberget*
by Rabén & Sjögren, 1986
Printed in Italy
First American edition, 1987

R & S Books are distributed in the United States by Farrar, Straus and Giroux, New York,
in the UK by Ragged Bears, Andover,
and in Canada by Methuen Publications, Toronto, Ontario.
ISBN 91 29 575907

Jens Ahlbom

JONATHAN OF GULL MOUNTAIN

Translated by Barbara Lucas

R&S
BOOKS

Stockholm   New York   Toronto   London

When Jonathan was born, he was the finest, most beautiful, smartest, and happiest boy there ever was. That's what his papa said.

"The boy is wonderful," said his mama. "He doesn't cry at night, and when I tickle him on the stomach, he laughs out loud."

"He's really going to be remarkable when he grows up," said Papa.

"A world-famous inventor or scientist or space explorer."

"Oh!" said Mama. "You always exaggerate. I'll be satisfied if he just is happy."

Jonathan himself doesn't remember much from that time. He remembers being just like all the other children.

Jonathan grew up in a house on Gull Mountain, high up near the clouds. There were many exciting places to play: the attic with all the old furniture and the cellar with its dark passageways. But Jonathan loved best of all to go with Mama or Papa on a flying trip. He loved to sit on their shoulders and feel the wind rushing through his hair, and the spinning sensation in his stomach when he looked down. Everything seemed so small and beautiful from above.

Sometimes they flew to the grocery store to shop. It was especially nice when Sara and her mother were there. Sara was Jonathan's best friend. They played hide-and-seek behind the shelves of canned goods and raced shopping carts in the aisles. One time Jonathan wrote a secret love letter to Sara with toothpaste on the floor! Of course, when Papa found out, it wasn't a secret anymore . . . or very pleasant either.

Sara and Jonathan were almost always together. One day Jonathan decided to build the world's highest tower with blocks. They pretended that Sara would move in and live there with him.

"We'll be able to look out over the whole world," said Sara.

"And feel how the tower sways. The winds blow very hard up here," said Jonathan. He put the last block on top. Right at that moment, he lost his balance and fell to the floor in a rain of blocks.

"Never mind!" said Jonathan, laughing. "We'll fly up to the clouds instead!"

"You're so silly!" Sara said. "You're always falling down. How do you expect to fly? You don't even have wings."

This hurt Jonathan's feelings. He had never thought much about not having wings. When he came home, he stood in front of the large mirror in the living room.

"Yes, it's true," he sighed. "Sara has wings. And Mama and Papa, too. Everyone has wings except me. I'll never learn to fly." It felt as if he had a large lump in his chest.

Mama took him on her knee and held him tight.

"Jonathan," she said, "life is not always easy. It can be very
difficult sometimes. Perhaps it is going to be even more difficult
for you because you have no wings. But you must learn to live
with that. Remember one important thing. You are just as good
and as important as everyone else. And we love you very
much!"

But on the day when all the children tried their wings for the first time, Jonathan couldn't help feeling miserable and left out.

All the children stood waiting for their turn, eager and happy.

One after the other, they sailed out over the edge of the cliff on unsteady wings, higher and higher in the clear air. Jonathan caught Sara's eye. She looked very unhappy and he began to feel that lump in his chest again.

13

The children spent the whole summer practicing their flying, all except Jonathan. When autumn came, school began, but Jonathan had to stay at home. How could he get to school? It was high up on a mountain, like all the other buildings. And now he was too big and heavy for Mama and Papa to fly with him on their shoulders.

Poor Jonathan! Never again would he be able to feel the wind rushing through his hair, or feel that wonderful spinning sensation in his stomach when he looked down on the earth from above.

He didn't have any friends to be with either. Sometimes he thought he heard the others whispering about him. They pointed at him when they flew by.

They think I am stupid just because I can't fly, he thought.

Only Sara came occasionally after school.

She probably plays with me only to be kind, thought Jonathan. She feels sorry for me!

Then he would shout, "Fly away from here! I want to be alone." But when she was gone, he was very lonely.

One morning he decided he had had enough. "I will not be pitied," he said to himself. "I am just as good as anybody else, and I have two legs. I will walk to school!"

It was not especially far away. Down the mountain, across the valley, over the river, and up on top of the next mountain. Jonathan gathered his books and wrote a note to his mother: I HAVE GON TO SCOOL.

But it was steep and difficult to climb down the mountain. He stepped on several loose stones, and it seemed as if the whole mountain came crashing down around him. He tripped and scraped both knees and one elbow.

"Why aren't there any steps here!" he shouted angrily into the air. Down below in the valley lay the river, broad and deep.

"Why isn't there a bridge?" asked Jonathan. "How am I going to get across? I might as well go back home again."

I HAVE GON TO SCOOL

Then he noticed a raft lying in the water. It was made of logs bound together with rope. There was a pole there too. What luck! And how fortunate that the river flowed slowly and there was no wind. He reached the other side easily. But the rocks and boulders made it difficult to get ashore. They hurt his feet.

"Why isn't there a road here?" Jonathan said, sighing. "I can't understand it."

But he gritted his teeth and continued, up one boulder, down the next, across the valley until he came to the foot of the mountain on which the school was perched.

There he stood, craning his neck, and stared. Far up above was the school, like a small impregnable fortress on top of a nearly vertical wall.

Jonathan didn't make a sound. He felt the lump in his chest begin to grow. He wanted to cry. Instead, he kicked a stone with all his might. It hit the mountain with a dull thud.

"I know how you feel," a voice said. "This place is not built for us."

Jonathan turned around. There stood a very old man looking at him. His face was as wrinkled as a dry plum, and Jonathan was a little afraid. But the old man looked friendly, and he had very kind eyes.

"Can't you fly either?" asked Jonathan, looking at him more closely. "You have wings like all the others."

"My wings are too weak nowadays," said the old man. "They don't hold me up any longer."

"And I thought that I was the only one in the whole world who couldn't fly," said Jonathan.

"Oh no, there are many of us," said the old man. "But we are not very noticeable. We live like shadows down here on the earth."

Jonathan was dumbfounded. He wasn't alone, after all!

"But if that's true, why are all the schools and houses and stores high up on the mountains?"

"Because it's always been like that," said the old man.

"But why hasn't anyone built steps and bridges and roads for those who can't fly?"

"Because the ones who make the decisions can't understand what it's like not to be able to fly," said the old man.

"Then we must explain it to them," said Jonathan. "After all, they, too, will become old and tired someday."

"You are a bright boy," said the old man, laughing. "But when those who make the decisions get old, then others begin to make the decisions. Come on, I'll walk home with you. I live on the other side of the river, just like you. It was my raft you borrowed. We can talk some more later. Now let's hurry so your mother won't be worried."

But Mama was already both worried and angry.

"Promise me that you will never again do such a dangerous thing," she scolded. "You could have been crushed, sliding down the mountain. And imagine if you had drowned in the river!" She hugged him close.

"There wasn't any danger," said Jonathan. "It was a fine raft. I just got my feet a little wet."

Sara was having a hard time in school. It was so empty and sad without Jonathan. He and Sara had always had such a good time together.

Smack! A paper airplane hit Sara, right on the nose. She jumped up. Behind her she heard a giggle. It was Krille.

"You bully. I'll fix you!" she shouted, picking up the paper plane. Then she had an idea — a great idea.

"Now I know how Jonathan can come to school!" she said to herself, and hugged the paper plane. When school was over, she raced to Jonathan's house to tell him about her plan.

He was digging steps down the mountain when she arrived. "Jonathan!" shouted Sara. "We can fix it so that you can fly!" She landed on a boulder and took the paper plane out of her school bag.

"Look!" she said. "We will build wings for you — like these, but bigger. Watch!"

She threw the paper plane out over the edge of the cliff.

"That's a wonderful idea!" said Jonathan. "That's a wonderful, fantastic idea!" His eyes shone. "I'm going to be able to fly!"

Sara nodded. They stood silently and watched the paper plane soaring on the wind until they could no longer see it. Then they took each other's hand and ran up to the house to tell Jonathan's parents.

That night Mama and Papa stayed up late. They were trying to decide what the wings should look like. It wasn't easy. They had to be big enough to carry Jonathan but not too heavy.

The next day was Saturday. Mama drew the pattern on some cloth. Sara's mother hemmed the pieces on the sewing machine. Sara and Jonathan helped Papa make a frame of lightweight aluminium rods.

Late that night the wings were finished. Red, gleaming wings on a sturdy frame of rods.

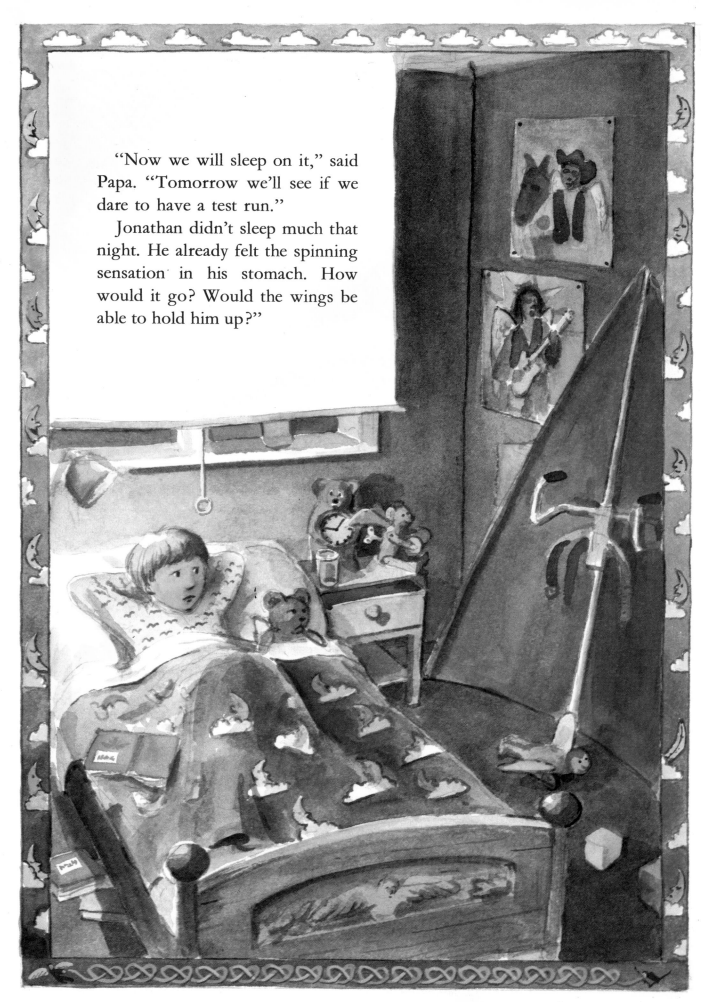

"Now we will sleep on it," said Papa. "Tomorrow we'll see if we dare to have a test run."

Jonathan didn't sleep much that night. He already felt the spinning sensation in his stomach. How would it go? Would the wings be able to hold him up?"

On the cliff where Sara had made her first flight, Jonathan attached his new wings. Papa stood at the edge holding a long rope which had been fastened around Jonathan's waist. They were going to fly together, for if Jonathan flew alone, he might crash down in the valley like the paper plane. But if someone flew with him and towed him on a line, he could fly like a kite, as long as he liked.

"Hold on. Now we're going to fly," shouted Papa. He leaped off the edge.

Jonathan ran a few yards behind him. He felt the wind filling the wings and lifting him up.

I am flying, he thought.

"I am flying!" he shouted. His voice echoed among the mountains, and people looked out of their houses to see what was happening.

Below Jonathan the river looked like a light blue ribbon. He thought about his difficult hike to the school.

We still need steps, a bridge, and a road, he thought. I will make sure, when I grow up, that they are built.

Look, I can steer, too! Up, down, and to the side, if I lean in different directions.

Then he made a perfect landing, right in the middle of his playmates. They applauded so loudly it was heard all over the valley.

"What did I say!" said Papa. "Didn't I say that he would be a remarkable boy? He is the only person in the world who has red wings. Look how they shine in the sun!"

"Tomorrow we will fly to school," whispered Sara. "Together."

And that's how it was. Sara and Jonathan. Jonathan and Sara. Best friends in rain or shine. Now they were flying to school together.

Krille turned up his nose when they came flying in.

"What a spectacle you make," he said to Jonathan. "What kind of crazy wings are those, anyhow?"

But it didn't matter, because it was so great to be with everyone again — to laugh and joke and tease. Sometimes it got to be too much for the teacher!

On the way home, Sara and Jonathan flew with the other children. High up in the air, they played jump rope among the clouds with Jonathan's towline.

In the house on Gull Mountain, Mama and Papa watched the children. "Look how much fun they're having," said Mama. "Now Jonathan is no longer alone."

If you should happen to fly by the house late some evening, you will see a light in the window. Jonathan and his papa are drawing and constructing. They are building something new. What do you suppose it will be?